HOORADE DAY!

The name Star Bright Books and the Star Bright Books logo are registered
trademarks of Star Bright Books, Inc. Please visit: www.starbrightbooks.com.
For bulk orders, please email: orders@starbrightbooks.com, or call customer
service at: (617) 354-1300.

Printed on paper from sustainable forests.

Hardback ISBN-13: 978-1-59572-807-4
Paperback ISBN-13: 978-1-59572-808-1
Star Bright Books / MA / 00106180
Printed in China / WKT / 9 8 7 6 5 4 3 2 1

Library of Congress Cataloging-in-Publication Data

Names: Day, Nancy Raines, author. | Van Wright, Cornelius, illustrator.
Title: Hoorade day! / Nancy Raines Day ; illustrated by Cornelius Van Wright.
Description: Cambridge, Massachusetts : Star Bright Books, [2018] | Summary:
  Illustrations and rhyming text reveal a young girl's view of her town's
  big Independence Day parade, and the family and friends participating in
  it, as seen from her father's shoulders.
Identifiers: LCCN 2018011147| ISBN 9781595728074 (hardcover) | ISBN
  1595728074 (hardcover) | ISBN 9781595728081 (pbk.) | ISBN 1595728082 (pbk.)
Subjects: | CYAC: Stories in rhyme. | Parades--Fiction. | Fourth of
  July--Fiction.
Classification: LCC PZ8.3.D3334 Hoo 2018 | DDC [E]--dc23
LC record available at https://lccn.loc.gov/2018011147

HOORADE DAY!

By
Nancy Raines Day

Illustrated by
Cornelius Van Wright

STAR BRIGHT BOOKS
CAMBRIDGE MASSACHUSETTS

Waking up. Hooray, hooray!
This will be a special day.

Pack some water, hats for shade.
We are off to the hoorade!

Lawn chair drill team. *Hup, hup, hup!*
"I can't see, Dad. Boost me up."

Babies, kids, and grownups, too.
All dressed up in red-white-blue.

I hear music. Here they come!
Bleating horns and banging drums.

My big brother's in the band.
I yell, "Hey, Sam! Here I am!"

Cars, trucks, bikes roll down the street.
Neighbors grin and throw us treats.

Wave our flags. Hooray, hooray!
Happy birthday, U-S-A!

Now come all the girls who twirl!
Arms are flying, ribbons swirl.

Dancers strut. It's Coralee!
Someday soon that could be me.

Sun is blazing. We're so hot!
Someone squirts us. Now we're not.

Horses marching, *clop, clip, clop.*
Oops, one's pooping, *plop, plop, plop.*

No more floats are coming now.
Is it over? Look—oh wow!

Long, long legs and tall, tall hat.
Who's the man who looks like that?

Sweeper truck comes, *chug, chug, chug.*
Now it's time for friends to hug.

Uncle Bob's that man in blue,
holding cars to let us through.

Let's go home for lemonade.

That sure was a great hoorade!